BULLYSAURUS
UNDER THE SEA

DAMON BURNARD

Hodder
Children's
Books

This book is dedicated to Mike Summerbee,
Francis Lee and Colin Bell

Copyright © 2000 Damon Burnard

First published in Great Britain in 2000 by
Hodder Children's Books

A Catalogue record for this book is available from the British Library.

ISBN 0340 74365 4

Printed and bound in Great Britain by
Guernsey Press, Guernsey, Channel Islands

Hodder Children's Books
A division of Hodder Headline
338 Euston Road
London NW1 3BH

Once upon a time, in a forest, on an island, in the middle of a sea, there lived a bunch of dinosaurs in happy harmony. Oh! And a space alien, too!

Terry Dactyl →

Dinah Saur

Zooble

Bullysaurus

Theo Saurus

Tyrone 'O' saurus

Dolores Saurus

Frank

CHAPTER ONE

One summer's morning, the dinosaurs awoke and decided that it was the perfect kind of day to go to the beach . . .

They gathered together all the things they needed, then off they went, along the sandy path through the forest that led to the seaside . . .

First they covered themselves in
oil so that their skin wouldn't burn.

Then Frank, Dolores and Theo
built sandcastles . . .

. . . Dinah and Tyrone played
volleyball . . .

. . . and Zooble and Terry snoozed
in the sunshine.

Bullysaurus, meanwhile, pushed the raft into the sea and jumped aboard.

Bully listened to the sea gently lapping around him, and to the distant, happy shouts of his friends on the shore.

Suddenly . . .

6

SPLASH!
SPLISH!
SPLASH!

A shoal of fish began playing
around him! They leapt high into the
air, then dived back down into the
sea.

Bully laughed and looked over
the side of the raft. The sea was
alive with fish!

In those days fish were a dull kind of greeny-browny-grey, but Bully gasped with wonder all the same.

"But how much more beautiful they'd be," he thought,

Bully closed his heavy eyelids and fell asleep dreaming of a sea filled with rainbow-coloured fish.

CHAPTER TWO

When Bully awoke he was shivering.
Grey clouds filled the sky, and a cold
wind whistled across the raft.

"Oh no!" whimpered Bully, looking
around him.

The shore – and his friends – had
all disappeared! He was surrounded
by water, as far as the eye could see!

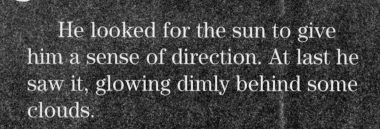

He looked for the sun to give him a sense of direction. At last he saw it, glowing dimly behind some clouds.

But the sun was no help at all. It was moving around the sky in a great big circle!

"What's happening?" groaned Bully, clutching his head.

And then he realised that it wasn't the sun that was moving . . .

Bully was circling around the edge of a huge whirlpool!

He paddled with all his might, but the current was too strong.

Round and round he went, in smaller and smaller circles, quicker and quicker all the time . . .

A deafening roar filled his ears, and icy foam fizzed around him. Bully clung to the raft with all his might. Faster and faster he whirled, and then . . .

. . . down he was sucked, down into the dark centre of the whirlpool!

CHAPTER THREE

When Bully opened his eyes he was lying on the raft, floating through a huge cave.

Mysterious rocks rose from the water and hung from the ceiling. The walls were encrusted with a million sparkling jewels. They lit up the cave like a million tiny suns.

"Wow!" gasped Bully.

The raft carried Bully into a second cave – as beautiful as the first.

But now Bully's heart sank.

"Oh, no!" he groaned. "This place goes on forever!"

When he thought about his island and his friends, a lump rose in his throat. But Bully refused to cry.

The river curved and twisted through corridors of stone and caves of gleaming jewels.

"It's no use!" Bully whimpered at last.

He'd just decided to cry, when suddenly . . .

He heard a voice! A feeble, distant voice!

"HELLO?" he called back.

At first there was silence . . .

. . . but then came a reply!
"Yes!" said the tiny voice.

Bully's heart leapt. He didn't
know who the voice belonged to, or
where it was coming from, but one
thing was for certain . . .

CHAPTER FOUR

As Bullysaurus steered the raft through the maze of caves, the voice grew slowly louder.

Bully turned a corner, and . . .

Before him, on a slab of rock, lay the skeleton of a huge monster!

Razor-like teeth lined its jaws, and on its hands shone deadly claws!

Shaking, Bully stepped off the raft and tiptoed over.

The monster's head was resting next to a pile of jewels. They were larger and brighter than those on the walls. He'd never seen such beautiful colours! Suddenly . . .

Bully jumped.

"Inside!" came the weary reply. "Please help!"

Nervously, Bully walked around the monster's head, past its neck, and down to its ribcage.

And that's where he found it, holding on to the ribs like the bars of a prison.

CHAPTER FIVE

Trapped inside the monster's ribcage was a strange creature. On his head was a beret, and from his chin grew a long, green beard. A frayed bag was slung over the shoulder of his old smock, and his ragged trousers barely covered his knees. His webbed feet were bare.

"Help at last!" he groaned, when he saw Bully. "After all these years!"

"Well, I'm Bullysaurus," said Bullysaurus. He reached through the monster's ribs and shook the sprite's pale, damp hand.

"Oh, it's an old, sad story . . ." sighed the sprite. "I'll tell it to you – if I can remember it. But first . . .

Bully said he'd do his best. He grabbed a rib in each hand and took a deep breath . . .

Bully pulled with all his might, and . . .

To his surprise, the ribs broke easily!

"Gosh!" said the sprite, quietly.
"That didn't look too hard."

He bowed politely to Bully.

The sprite stretched and sighed,
while Bully gathered together some
driftwood and built a fire.

"Yes," sniffed the sprite, "a little."
"Well, I'm starving!" Bully groaned.

The sprite dipped his beard into the river. . .

When he pulled it out, six
wriggling fish were caught there!

He tossed them to Bully, who
cooked them over the fire.

Bully ate three whole fish in the
time it took the sprite to nibble a
tail.

After he'd licked the bones clean, Bully turned to his companion.

So, now can you tell me how you got stuck inside the monster?

"Indeed I can," said the sprite, wiping his mouth.

So please make yourself comfortable and I will tell you of the terrible misfortunes which landed me in this place...

CHAPTER SIX

"Once upon a time," began the sprite, "a very long time ago, the Creator made the World."

First, the Creator built the hills and mountains, and filled the gaps between with sea. Then he made every living thing: the plants and animals, the birds and the fish.

There was much work to do, and the Creator had many helpers: pixies, fairies, imps, nymphs, and sprites – like me!

Some made feathers for the birds, others made leaves for the trees. My job was to colour the creatures of the sea.

The sprite felt in his bag and pulled out a palette and three brushes.

"But the fairy who'd painted the butterflies and birds had used up all the good colours!" he said.

For many years I painted the sea's creatures with that gloomy colour. But I could not help imagining how much more beautiful they'd be if they were painted the colours of the rainbow.

"Yes!" agreed Bully.

Now, that would be beautiful!

Sigh! I thought so once, too!

The sprite told Bully how an ancient octopus had told him of a world of caves under the sea. In one of them lived a fierce monster, who jealously guarded a pile of brightly-coloured jewels.

At once I set off to find this world. I planned to take the jewels, grind them up, and make paint from them. That way, I thought, I could make the oceans alive with colour!

For a hundred years I searched in vain. Then, just as I'd given up hope, a terrible whirlpool sucked me down to an undersea world – the world the octopus had told me of, all those years ago.

I made my way through caves and corridors and chambers. At last I came upon the monster. Even though it was sleeping, it was a terrible sight. I wanted to flee, but when I saw the jewels I remembered my dream and changed my mind.

I stepped bravely forward.

Carefully I placed a jewel in my bag, and then another. But as I reached for a third . . .

. . . the monster awoke!

I tried casting a magic spell to send it back to sleep, but my magic had no power so far beneath the sea.

With one lunge of its terrible head, the monster swallowed me whole!

I lived in the monster's belly for years and years, never knowing if it was night or day.

At first I struggled to escape, but it was no use. After a while I stopped trying. I sat in darkness instead, and I began to regret the dream that had brought me there . . .

"At last the monster died, and its flesh rotted away," said the sprite.

CHAPTER SEVEN

"Wow!" gasped Bully.

Bully told the sprite how he, too, had been sucked down by the whirlpool. "I was looking for a way out," he said, "when I found you!"

"Goody! Now we can search together!" said the sprite. He jumped on to the raft.

"But wait!" said Bully. "What about the jewels? And the rainbow-coloured fish?"

"Are you crazy?" replied the sprite. "I tried once, and look what happened."

The sprite studied the monster's bones.

"I'm not so sure," he said gravely.

"It's too dangerous," replied the sprite.

"But imagine a sea of rainbow-coloured fish!" insisted Bully. "Isn't it worth the risk?"

The sprite fell silent and thoughtfully tugged at his beard.

For the first time since they'd met, the sprite's eyes twinkled. He leapt off the raft and ran over to Bully.

Bully looked at the monster and gulped nervously. "Y – yes!" he said, after a while.

Now the sprite's eyes blazed like suns.

CHAPTER EIGHT

Bullysaurus and the sprite stood over the jewels. The sprite took a deep breath.

He took a sparkling emerald and placed it in his bag.
The monster's head shifted.

"No," said the sprite, even though he had.

Next, Bully took a giant ruby.

The monster's hand made a fist! "Did you see that?" asked Bully.

"Y – yes," said the sprite, though he wished he hadn't.

Bully and the sprite heaped jewels into the bag as fast as they could.

With each handful the monster moved, as if it was waking from a deep sleep . . .

At last the bag was full.

Bully jumped on to the raft, while the sprite fumbled with his hat and bag.

Suddenly . . .

The sprite scrambled on to the raft. Hurriedly, they pushed off into the river . . .

"What were you doing?" panted
Bully.

"Never mind that now!" shouted
the sprite.

Bully looked over his shoulder.
To his horror the monster had risen
to its feet and was stepping into the
river.

CHAPTER NINE

Bully and the sprite paddled as fast as they could, but with each passing second, the monster gained on them . . .

Through caves and passageways they raced. The river was moving faster now; it fizzed and foamed about the raft as it swept them along . . .

Bully steered around some jagged rocks. "If the monster doesn't get us!" he panted,

...the rocks will!

To try and lose the monster Bully and the sprite twisted and turned down tunnels and passageways . . .

Gradually the monster's roars grew distant. Then, at last, it was silent.

Bully looked over his shoulder. "It's given up!" he cried, as the raft hurtled around the corner.

Suddenly . . .

CHAPTER TEN

Bully and the sprite rose spluttering to the surface.

"Oh my goodness!" gasped Bully.

Rising up before them was an incredible sight; a twisting, turning tower of water!

Suddenly . . .

"No, it's not us he wants!" bellowed the sprite, tearing off his bag.

The sprite hurled the bag into the foaming tower of water.

The monster roared with rage.

The sprite and Bully fell from its grasp, as the monster leapt after the bag . . .

But the powerful whirlpool was too much for the monster . . .

A tumbling jumble of bones span up the whirlpool . . .

. . . and out through a hole in the cave's roof!

CHAPTER ELEVEN

"But what about the jewels?" said Bully sadly. "And our dream?"

"They're quite safe!" chuckled the sprite, taking off his hat.

The inside of his hat was brimming with gleaming, multi-coloured jewels!

"I swapped them for pebbles, just after we took them," the sprite explained . . .

"That was clever!" said Bully,

"But we have!" said the sprite, pointing to the whirlpool.

"Because we're alive, and we've got a dream," said the sprite.

Over they swam, into the whirlpool . . .

They took a deep breath, and . . .

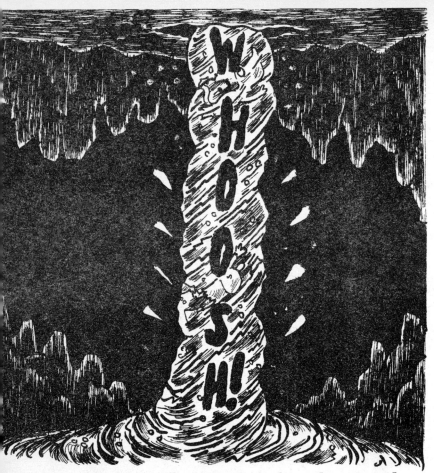

Up they flew, around and around, twisting and turning, head over heels . . .

And that was the last thing that Bully remembered . . .

CHAPTER TWELVE

Bullysaurus awoke. He was lying on his raft in the sunshine, floating in the sea.

Bully looked up.

It was Dolores and the others, calling from the shore!

"W – what?" gasped Bully, as he paddled ashore.

Bully stepped onto the sand, and his friends gathered around him.

"Did you fall asleep?" asked Dolores.

"Y – yes," said Bully. "I suppose I must have."

Bully told them about the whirlpool, the monster and the dream he shared with the sea-sprite.

"But I don't understand . . ." he said, sadly shaking his head.

Suddenly . . .

Leaping from the sea came a
shoal of flying fish!

But these fish weren't a dull kind
of greeny-browny-grey . . .

"It's him!" laughed Bully, remembering what the sprite had told him about his gift of magic.

And Bully's friends laughed, too – with joy and wonder at the incredible sight. For they believed in Bully, and they believed in magic, and they believed in dreams coming true . . .

To this day, Bully's friend is painting fish with all the colours of the rainbow. He hasn't got round to doing all the fish yet, but if you visit an aquarium, or snorkel in a tropical sea, you'll see his colourful creations.

Once in a while, he trims his green beard so his brushes don't get tangled in it. You'll find the trimmings on the shore, when the tide goes out . . .

. . . and maybe a few of the monster's bones, as well!